P9-CMY-184

For Katie, Sophie, and Sam —M. W.
For Team "de Grey" —S. V.

Ω

Published by
PEACHTREE PUBLISHERS
1700 Chattahoochee Avenue
Atlanta, Georgia 30318-2112
www.peachtree-online.com

Text © 2009 by Martin Waddell
Illustrations © 2009 by Susan Varley

First published in Great Britain in 2009 by Andersen Press Ltd.
First United States edition published in 2010 by Peachtree Publishers

Illustrations created in pen and ink

Color separated in Switzerland by Photolitho AG, Zürich.
Printed and bound in January 2010 by Tien Wah Press in Singapore.

10   9   8   7   6   5   4   3   2   1

Library of Congress Cataloging-in-Publication Data

Waddell, Martin.
   Captain Small Pig / written by Martin Waddell ; illustrated by Susan Varley.
      p. cm.
   Summary: Small Pig and his friends Old Goat and Turkey spend the day in a row-
boat on a lake.
      ISBN: 978-1-56145-519-5 / 1-56145-519-9
   [1. Boats and boating--Fiction. 2. Pigs--Fiction. 3. Goats--Fiction. 4. Turkeys--Fiction.]
I. Varley, Susan, ill. II. Title.
   PZ7.W1137Cap 2010
   [E]--dc22
                                                          2009024992

CAPTAIN
SMALL PIG

Martin Waddell   Susan Varley

PEACHTREE
ATLANTA

One day Old Goat and Turkey took Small Pig down to Blue Lake. They found a little red boat.

"I want to go for a row!" Small Pig said, dancing about.

"Turkeys don't go in boats," Turkey said.

"Neither do goats," said Old Goat, but he climbed into the boat, and they rowed off onto Blue Lake.

"I want to fish for whales!" said Small Pig.

"There aren't any whales in Blue Lake," said Turkey.

"There might be a very small whale," said Old Goat, and he tied a string to an oar so Small Pig could try his whale fishing.

Small Pig didn't catch any whales, but he caught an old boot, which was almost as good.

"I want to row now!" said Small Pig.

"You're too small to row," Turkey objected.

"Of course you can row," said Old Goat.

Small Pig could only manage one oar at a time so he rowed...

round and round...

...round and round...round and round...

but he rowed the boat all by himself.

"I'm Captain Commander!" Small Pig said.
Turkey just shook his head sleepily.
"Aye aye, Captain Small Pig!" said Old Goat. "You are
in charge of this boat."

"But I'm too tired to row any more!" Small Pig said.

"I knew you would be," said Turkey.

"Just let the boat drift," said Old Goat, yawning.

"But keep your hand on the tiller..."

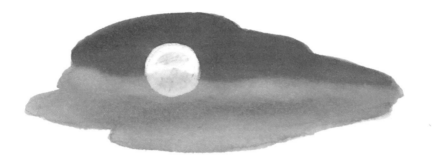

As the moon rose, the boat drifted back through the reeds, toward the shore.

Small Pig was...sort of...steering the boat.
And then...Small Pig...sort of...wasn't steering the boat.
He'd fallen asleep holding his boot.

The boat was...sort of...steering itself.

"My turn to steer," sighed
old Goat. He took over the
tiller and guided them back
to the dock.

As they drew near, Old Goat rose out of his seat to tie up the boat.

It rocked...

one way...

and then the other...until...

I knew this would happen!" spluttered Turkey.

"*Shhhhh!* We mustn't wake up Captain Small Pig!" Old Goat warned Turkey.

They carried Small Pig all the way home, wrapped warm in a blanket, and they tucked him cozily into bed.

Small Pig slept...and he dreamed...of a lovely day out
in a boat with good friends on Blue Lake...

...the day that he was Captain Small Pig.